# THE SIGN PAINTER

## Allen Say

HOUGHTON MIFFLIN COMPANY BOSTON 2000

Walter Lorraine Books

Walter Lorraine (wl) Books

Library of Congress Cataloging-in-Publication Data

Say, Allen.
  The Sign Painter / by Allen Say
p. c.m.
Summary: An assignment to paint a large billboard in the desert changes the life
of an aspiring artist.
  ISBN 0-395-97974-9
  [1. Artists — Fiction. 2. Signs and signboards — Fiction.]
I. Title.
PZ7 .S2744Si          2000 [Fic] — dc21

Printed in the United States of America
WOZ  10  9  8  7  6  5  4  3  2  1

For Emi Oshima

That morning, only one passenger got off the early bus.

He seemed quite young, rubbing his eyes as though trying to shake off sleep or find out where he was. He looked down the empty street with dark storefronts on both sides and gave a sigh. Not even the coffee shop was open. Then he turned the other way, where the bus had gone, and saw a lighted window two blocks away. He crossed the street.

When he came to it, he saw that it was a sign shop, and through the window he could see a man working inside. He hesitated, then straightened and tapped on the glass. The man looked up, stared for a moment, and beckoned with a nod. The young man walked in.

"Are you lost, son?" the man asked.

"Yes . . . I mean no. I need a job," the young man stammered, looking not much more than a boy.

"Tell me what you can do."

"I can paint."

"Ah, an artist. Are you good at faces?"

"I think so."

"Can you paint them big?"

"Yes."

"All right, I'm interested." The man put down the brush and said, "Come with me."

7

They drove to a vacant lot where a blank billboard had been set up.

"This is your model," the man said, showing the boy a picture of a woman. "I want her on the right, as big as you can make her."

The boy worked quickly; he outlined a face taller than himself and then began to paint. At lunchtime the man said, "You seem to know what you're doing."

In the late afternoon, a large white car drove up. As the sign painter walked toward it, the back window rolled down, and he spoke to someone inside. After a while, an envelope was handed to him, and the car drove away.

He was flushed when he said to the boy, "How would you like to work on a dozen billboards?"

They started out early the following morning.

"We'll be working in the desert," the man said.

"I like painting landscapes," the boy said.

"You're painting a woman, just the way the layout shows. Goes with one word, ArrowStar. That's it."

"What is ArrowStar?"

"I didn't ask," replied the man.

By midafternoon they were driving into the desert.

Later that day they came to the first job site.

"Now, there's a canvas for you," the man said.

"It'll be like painting a mural," the boy said. "But who's going to see it way out here?"

"That's not our problem," the man said.

13

They spent three days on the first board and moved on to the next. They set up a tent and cooked their beans over a fire.

"How does it feel to be a wage earner?" the man asked.

"I am a painter," the boy replied.

"We all have dreams. What made you want to paint?"

"It's what I love."

"But you found out you had to make a living."

"Yes."

"We'll make a good team. You won't go hungry."

The boy did not answer.

As time went on, they spoke less, as if their voices would disturb the silence around them. Only the landscape changed. Then one day the boy said, "How many more?"

"Are you tired?" the man asked.

"I'm not tired."

"What's bothering you then?"

"I keep wondering, who'll know the difference if I put mountains in the background, even just a cloud?"

"Son, when someone pays you to paint a woman, will you give him a landscape?"

The boy looked away.

They went on, setting up and breaking down the tent, moving on to yet another blank signboard. So the morning when the man announced, "One more to go," the boy said, "One more what?" The man laughed.

But a wind came up, and they were caught in a raging dust storm. They rolled up the windows and spent the night sitting up in the truck.

Sometime before dawn the wind died. The man turned the ignition, and as the engine sputtered to life, they sighed with relief. But when the last billboard came into sight, they rubbed their blurry eyes. Only the skeleton of it was left standing. The panels had been blown away and were nowhere to be seen.

"I don't know if we can fix this," he grumbled.

The boy looked off toward the horizon.

"Watch out!" the boy shouted. The man leapt backward. The swerving car barely missed him.

"It's the ArrowStar woman!" the boy cried.

"What is she doing out here?"

"She came from those towers."

"Couldn't be oil wells. Let's have a look."

Approaching the looming towers, the man said,
"That must be ArrowStar."

"What can they be?" the boy asked.

The man stepped hard on the brakes. "It's a roller coaster!"

They stared in silence. Then the boy pointed at a smaller mesa,
which had houses on top. "But why out here?" he asked.

"I wonder," the man said. "Maybe that road will lead
to the answer."

They drove on, staring in amazement at the sight before them. An immense curtain hung in the sky, and under that a cluster of houses nested on a rock as if floating on a cloud. From there a long ramp sloped down to the desert floor.

The man eased the truck onto the ramp. They pulled into a lot at the top and got out. The boy followed the man onto the narrow streets. They peered into gaping windows of empty houses with not a single piece of furniture inside. The only sound came from their footsteps.

Suddenly they stopped.

Someone was talking nearby. The man put his finger to his lips, and the two followed the voice to an open archway.

". . . imagine it, all lit up at night . . ." A man in a white suit was talking on the telephone. "Had the name for years, before any of the building was done . . . the whole thing was riding on the highway coming through . . . who knows? But we'll advertise . . . billboards . . . we can only hope . . . no, she left — couldn't wait, she said . . ."

The sign painter pulled the boy away from the archway.

They coasted down the ramp. Neither said a word until ArrowStar was behind them.

"Will he succeed?" the man asked.

"I hope so," the boy answered.

"Goes to show that dreams come in all sizes. But we're done, for now. How do you feel about working with me?"

The boy said nothing.

"Look, there's the cloud you wanted to paint — even has a frame around it."

The boy turned to look.

"There it goes, just passing by, like you and me. And the builder of ArrowStar, good luck to him."

The next day, before sunset, they were back in the shop.

It was late when the boy said good-bye to the sign painter. And as the last bus came around the corner he said softly to the empty street, "Just passing by . . ."